You Can't take an Elephant on HOLIDAY

Patricia Cleveland-Peck

Illustrated by

David Tazzyman

BLOOMSBURY
CHILDREN'S BOOKS
LONDON   OXFORD   NEW YORK   NEW DELHI   SYDNEY

You can't take an **elephant** on holiday . . .

He'd spoil your fun and get in the way.
You'd see him shove to the front of the queue,
eat ALL the ice cream, and leave none for you!

A **cheetah** in charge of a **camper van**
is something they really ought to ban . . .

Speed is a thing she simply adores —
but the rules of the road
she ALWAYS ignores.

If an **ostrich** wants some sun and fresh air,
don't let her near an old **deckchair** . . .

She'll put it up badly and make it collapse,
so it's most unlikely she'll get to relax.

Don't lend your **surfboard** to an **orangutan** . . .

She can, in fact, do most things YOU can.
So it won't take her long to get the knack
and you probably won't get your surfboard back.

A **rhino** on a **campsite** would cause a to-do . . .

He'd put all the tents up completely askew.
He'd get in a mood, he'd get in a rage
and charge round the campsite on the rampage.

Meerkats are such an unruly mob,
playing **mini-golf** with them is quite a job . . .

With a clutter of putters and balls whizzing past,
if you ever opt in, you'll opt out pretty fast.

SANDCASTLE CONTEST TODAY

Don't let an **armadillo** give you a hand
when you're building a **castle** made of **sand** . . . .

She'll dig right down and burrow deep —
and your castle will end up

in a

heap!

And it's best to hide from the **albatross**

when trying to eat your **candyfloss** . . .

She can't resist anything sticky and sweet,

so if you spot her — take to your feet.

A **bison?** On a *pedalo?* A VERY weird sight . . .

He'd happily pedal with all his might.
But should he drift into the main shipping lane,
he'd soon realise that his jaunt was insane.

Paddling in a pool with **piranha fish**

would be a CRAZY thing to wish . . .

With razor-sharp teeth just made to bite,
they're sure to give you a nasty fright.

A **lion** as a **tour guide** just wouldn't work,
he'd drive all the passengers quite beserk . . .

And if he gave them a welcoming ROAR,
they'd all get up and stampede for the door.

"We just **want** to have **fun**,"
the animals say.
"But we **always** seem
to get in the **way**."

Well, who needs a paddling pool

or a deckchair,

when YOU can

enjoy . . .

All the **FUN** of the **FAIR!**

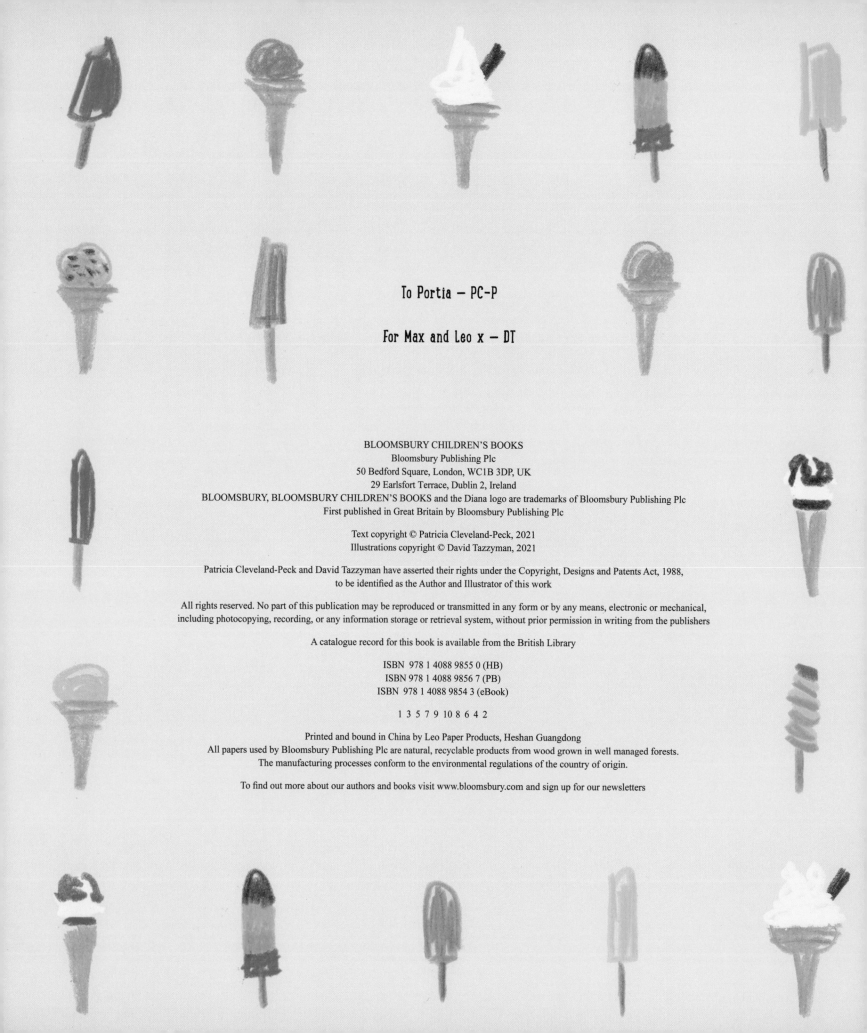

To Portia — PC-P

For Max and Leo x — DT

BLOOMSBURY CHILDREN'S BOOKS
Bloomsbury Publishing Plc
50 Bedford Square, London, WC1B 3DP, UK
29 Earlsfort Terrace, Dublin 2, Ireland
BLOOMSBURY, BLOOMSBURY CHILDREN'S BOOKS and the Diana logo are trademarks of Bloomsbury Publishing Plc
First published in Great Britain by Bloomsbury Publishing Plc

Text copyright © Patricia Cleveland-Peck, 2021
Illustrations copyright © David Tazzyman, 2021

Patricia Cleveland-Peck and David Tazzyman have asserted their rights under the Copyright, Designs and Patents Act, 1988,
to be identified as the Author and Illustrator of this work

A catalogue record for this book is available from the British Library

ISBN 978 1 4088 9855 0 (HB)
ISBN 978 1 4088 9856 7 (PB)
ISBN 978 1 4088 9854 3 (eBook)

1 3 5 7 9 10 8 6 4 2

Printed and bound in China by Leo Paper Products, Heshan Guangdong
All papers used by Bloomsbury Publishing Plc are natural, recyclable products from wood grown in well managed forests.
The manufacturing processes conform to the environmental regulations of the country of origin.

To find out more about our authors and books visit www.bloomsbury.com and sign up for our newsletters